Dennis finds
a new job

Dennis Dragon was quite happy
Working in the baker's shop,
Making bread and buns and
   crumpets —
From morning until night, non-stop.

But one day the baker told him,
"I won't need you any more,
For my son is coming home and
He can turn out cakes galore.

He has been to Baker's College
And has a certificate.
He can make all kinds of goodies.
He'll be my new baker's mate."

Dennis
the Dragon

written by JUNE WOODMAN
and RITA GRAINGE

illustrated by MARTIN AITCHISON

*After leaving Dragon school Dennis finds a job with a
baker. But after a while Dennis finds himself without a
job. Having tried the zoo and an ice-cream factory, he
settles down as the train driver at a fun fair. All is well
until he becomes very unhappy and begins to look for a
wife – which turns out to be not as easy as it sounds!
A delightful, full colour, humorous sequel to* Dennis the
Dragon, *told in rhyme, to delight all young children.*

First edition

© LADYBIRD BOOKS LTD MCMLXXXIII 4/3/91

5

Dennis couldn't quite believe that
He was being asked to go.
But he packed his few belongings
And he set off, feeling low.

Dennis went from town to town in
Search of something he could do.
But he found, to his great sorrow,
Jobs for dragons were *very* few.

"No one wants a baker dragon,"
Whimpered Dennis with a sigh.
Then a notice on a window
Caught our dragon's tearful eye.

There, in letters bold and cheerful,
JOB CENTRE it plainly said.
"That's for me!" our Dennis shouted
And inside he quickly sped.

Then the man behind the desk said,
"We can find a job for you —
We can help all kinds of people,
Tell me just what you can do."

"I can do a lot," said Dennis,
Puffing out his chest with pride.
"In that case," smiled Mr Jolly,
"You can do a Dragon Ride."

DRAGON
RIDES
HERE

10

So it was that Dennis Dragon
Ended up inside the Zoo,
Giving rides to little children
Like the elephants all do.

But the elephants were rounder;
Dennis had a *spiky* back.
All the children were complaining
That their bottoms were blue and
  black.

ELEPHANT
RIDES

DRAGON
RIDES

Monday morning saw poor Dennis
In the line of unemployed.
"Back so soon?" asked Mr Jolly,
Sounding really quite annoyed.

But he found a job for Dennis

As a factory guard at night;

He would watch for thieves and robbers;

He would give them such a fright.

13

Everything went well at first and
Dennis made a splendid guard.
No one dared to break and enter,
All the gates stayed locked and
    barred.

Then one night a most tremendous
CRASH and BANG our Dennis heard,
Coming from inside the warehouse —
But 'our hero' was prepared!

Breathing fire . . . and flames . . . and
    fury
Into battle Dennis sprang —
"I will teach those thieves a lesson!
I'll make mincemeat of their gang!"

Bursting through the door he puffed
  out

Giant flames from side to side.

"No one can escape from this — I'll

Be a HERO!" Dennis cried.

Peering through the smoke and ashes
Dennis searched this way and that.
All he found inside the warehouse
Was one frightened little CAT!

Suddenly the cat began to
Lap up something off the floor;
White and pink and chocolate puddles
Trickled out beneath the door.

Chocolate, strawberry and vanilla —
Dennis stood there in a dream.
What a stupid little Dragon,
Using flames to guard ICE-CREAM!

Once again on Monday morning
Dennis queued up with the rest.
''GO AWAY!'' yelled Mr Jolly,
''You've become a perfect PEST.''

Sadly, once again poor Dennis
Went on his way, bowed down with
care.
He kept on walking, then at tea-time
Found himself outside the Fair.

Helter-skelters, lots of music —
Lucky-dips in tubs of bran —
Everyone seemed very happy
All except for one poor man.

He was standing by the engine
Of his model railway train.
"What's the matter?" asked young Dennis,
"Are you ill? Are you in pain?"

Then the man explained, "This morning
Our coal truck just hasn't come,
And without a head of steam up
Little engines cannot run."

Shyly then, our jaunty hero
Went into action once again.
"I can help you, Mr Train Man,
I can drive the model train!"

23

"Don't be silly," said the owner.
"Coal's what I need for my train."
"I'll soon show you," promised Dennis,
Breathing fire with might and main.

Crouching down inside the cabin
Dennis made that boiler steam –
Slow at first, then ever faster
The little train went like a dream.

THE POETRY LIBRARY

Scores of happy little children
Climbed aboard with shouts of glee.
Dennis chuckled as he drove them,
"This is just the life for me!"

Dennis
gets married

Dennis was a kindly dragon
And he found it lots of fun
Giving rides to little children,
On the Model Railway run.

But as weeks turned into months and
Months turned into several years,
Dennis Dragon grew dejected –
Sighing sighs and shedding tears.

TICKETS

29

"What is *wrong* with you?" the train
man

Asked him one day, in despair.

"You're upset, and sad and gloomy.

It's no fun now, at the fair."

"I don't know," replied poor Dennis,

Looking all cross-eyed and glum.

"You must need a rest," the man said.

"Get off home and see your Mum."

31

So the dreary dragon started
Out for home, still filled with gloom.
He was met with love and kindness,
Put to bed in his old room.

But in spite of all Mum's efforts
He stayed weary, sad and blue.
Then his Mother told him firmly,
"I know what is wrong with you!

You are now a grown-up dragon,
Handsome, strong and full of pride.
You need someone sweet and gentle —
As a girlfriend, then a bride."

35

Dennis Dragon blushed bright green —
and

Then he blushed bright pink and red.

He was shy of lady dragons,

But he did what his Mum said.

Next day, in the local paper

There appeared in letters bold,

''WANTED — one bride for a dragon —

Must be kind, and good as gold.''

But, as Dennis rose and looked out
From his window one fine day,
He saw something most alarming
And was filled with great dismay.

Rushing up and down the pathway
Green and yellow, pink or blue
Dragon Ladies pushed and jostled
As they tried to jump the queue!

"I was first!" one dragon grumbled.

"No you WEREN'T!" there came
a shout.

As they pushed and shoved and
quarrelled,

Here and there a fight broke out.

Snappy dragons, tall ones, short ones,
Some were fat, and some too thin.
Biffing, banging, pushing, barging,
Some fell out, and some gave in.

All that day the battle raged as
Dennis watched, quite safe inside,
"But," he told his worried Mother,
"None of THEM will be my bride!"

Mother Dragon was determined
And told Dennis what to do.
"Send your facts to the computer.
It will find the girl for you."

So, at the computer centre
Dennis turned up, eyes aglow;
Popped his card into the slot, then
Pushed the button labelled GO.

GO

Bells and whistles, bleeps and buzzers,
Lights in yellow, green and red,
Dragons shot from the computer
Like a toaster popping bread!

15

Dennis looked at each new lady,
Viewed them all, but fancied none.
He went back home in disappointment;
Computer Dragons were no fun.

Dainty Daisy (next-door-neighbour),
Young and slim and looking great,
Turned to smile at Dennis, as he
Stopped beside his Mother's gate.

Dennis hadn't seen sweet Daisy
Since they were at Dragon School.
Now she really was a beauty;
Dennis almost lost his cool.

"What a lady!" thought our hero.
Shyly he held out his hand.
Daisy took it, and in no time
A summer wedding they had planned.

49

As they left the church together,

Dennis led the way with pride.

Who'd have thought his next-door-
     neighbour

Would turn out to be his bride.